Jules

Jacques

Jean

SIX FOOLISH FISHERMEN

Ti-Paul

ROBERT D. SAN SOUCI

Illustrated by
DOUG KENNEDY

HYPERION BOOKS FOR CHILDREN
New York

Pierre

Philippe

First Edition
1 3 5 7 9 10 8 6 4 2
The artwork was prepared using acrylic on velum.
This book is set in 16-point Celestia Antiqua.
Printed in Hong Kong by South China Printing Company, Ltd.
Library of Congress Cataloging-in-Publication Data
San Souci, Robert D.
Six foolish fishermen / Robert D. San Souci ; illustrated by Doug Kennedy.—1st ed.
p.   cm.
Summary: Six silly friends spend a day trying to figure out how to proceed with their fishing trip when one thing after another goes wrong.
ISBN 0-7868-0385-1 (trade : alk. paper).—ISBN 0-7868-2335-6 (lib. : alk. paper)
[1. Cajuns—Folklore. 2. Folklore—Louisiana.] I.Kennedy, Doug, ill. II. Title.
PZ8. 1. S227Sl   2000
[398.2'089'410763]—dc21

Visit www.hyperionchildrensbooks.com, a part of the GO Network

To My Very Dear Friend
Coleen C. Salley
Scholar, Storyteller, and
Once & Future
"Cajun Queen of New Orleans"

—R. D. S.

To my mom,
who cooks gumbo that's so delish!

—D. K.

Down in the bayou country of Louisiana there once lived six friends named Jules, Jacques, Jean, Ti-Paul, Philippe, and Pierre. They loved to go fishing together. They would take their six little pirogues out onto the bayou at sunrise and fish for barbue or bass or *sac-à-lait* until sunset.

They would sing:

> A *little piece of pepper*
> In *the gumbo made with fish,*
> *That a thing that's good—*
> *That a thing delish!*

But one morning, when the friends got to the bank of the bayou, they found that three of them—Ti-Paul, Philippe, and Pierre—had brought their fishing poles, but no bait. The other three—Jules, Jacques, and Jean—had remembered to bring bait, but forgot their fishing poles. "*Mais non!* We are too foolish, us!" cried Jules. "Now none of us can go fishin', 'cause there en't one of us has both a pole and bait."

They were about to return home, when an old *grandmaman* came along the path. She carried an empty basket and was on her way to town. She heard the friends talking, and said to them, "You don't gotta end the day 'fore it begin. The fellas with fishin' poles oughtta give 'em to the fellas with bait; or the fellas with bait oughtta give it to the fellas with poles. One way or 'nother, three of you can be fishin'."

She continued on her way.

But Pierre said, "Why can only three men be fishin'? If three of us give our bait to the fellas who got poles, then three can be fishin'. If three of us give our fishin' poles to the fellas who got bait, then three more can be fishin'. Since three and three make six, all of us can be fishin'!"

So the three men with bait handed it to the other three. At the same time, the three men who had fishing poles handed them to their friends.

But now Jules, Jacques, and Jean had fishing poles, but no bait, while Ti-Paul, Philippe, and Pierre had bait, but no fishing poles.

"That foolish old woman!" cried Pierre. "Well, even if we can't fish, we can still row out and eat breakfast. That the best part of fishin' ennyhow; an' I'm hungry, me."

So the six anchored their pirogues on the water. But to their dismay, they found that Ti-Paul, Philippe, and Pierre had brought only crawfish pies, while Jules, Jacques, and Jean had brought only flasks of coffee. They began to cry because none of them could have a proper breakfast of crawfish pies and coffee.

At that moment, the *grandmaman* returned along the bayou path. When she heard the men complaining, she shouted to them, "If the three of you with pies give to the ones with coffee, and the three with coffee give to the ones with pies, you can all have a fine ol' meal."

Then she went on her way.

Philippe said, "Let's try what the ol' woman tol' us, though she was wrong before, her."

So Jules, Jacques, and Jean gave their flasks of coffee to their friends; and Ti-Paul, Philippe, and Pierre handed over their pies. But the result was that three of them still had nothing but coffee, while three had only pies.

"We mus' never listen to that ol' woman again!" cried Pierre. "She crazy, her!"

Since the day was now spoiled, they decided to return to shore and go home. But Ti-Paul suddenly leaned over the side of his skiff and carved an "X" with his scaling knife.

"What you doin'?" asked Pierre.

"This look like a good fishin' place," said Ti-Paul. "So I mark the spot to find it again."

Pierre roared with laughter. "Ti-Paul, you goose head, you! Suppose you don't be able to come here tomorrow. How the rest of us gonna find this place?"

"I didn' think of that," admitted Ti-Paul, scratching his head.

"Lucky for everyone, I smart-smart," said Pierre, tapping the side of his head with his finger. "*Mes amis*, my frien's," he called to the others, "we all gonna mark this place, so we can find it ennytime."

He carved an "X" on the side of his pirogue, and the others marked their boats also. Satisfied that they could each find the spot again, they rowed to shore.

But when they had drawn their pirogues onto the bank, Pierre said, "We mus' count ourse'fs, to be sure we all safe!"

So they lined up, while Pierre counted one-two-three-four-five. Because he didn't include himself, he exclaimed, "I only count five: one of us missin' and musta got drownded!"

The friends were very upset. At first they couldn't believe it, but each took a turn counting. And each failed to include himself, so they always counted five, not six, fishermen.

They all dived again and again into the bayou to look for their lost friend. But each time they came out, whoever chanced to count found only five wet fishermen.

"I sure don't see nobody in the water," said Jacques. "Mebbe a gator got him."

"I don't see no gator," said Jules.

"Well, if we don't see them both," said Jean, "that prove a gator et our frien' and the gator got gone. No use searchin' ennymore."

Then Pierre said, "Now we know one of us got hisse'f et by a gator. But we can't go home 'til we figger out who got et. I gonna point to each of you, and you say your name. That way, we can find who en't here."

One by one, he pointed to the men. In turn, they called out: "Jules," "Jacques," "Jean," "Ti-Paul," and "Philippe."

"Did ennyone call Pierre's name?" asked Pierre.

The other five shook their heads.

"Oh, oh, oh!" he cried. "If none of you call 'Pierre', then it mus' be me fall in the bayou and get et up."

"*Pauvre* Pierre!" cried the others. "Poor Pierre!"

The five friends laid Pierre down on an old blanket from Ti-Paul's boat. Then they sat weeping for their friend who had to be numbered among the dead because he had not been counted among the living.

While they were mourning, Pierre's wife, Henriette, came looking for him.

"Pierre! What you doin'?" she demanded.

"Silly woman!" her husband said, without opening his eyes. "How I can answer when I'm dead and et?"

"You gettin' crazy in the head?" she exclaimed. "How you can be dead when you talkin' to me?"

But he refused to say another word to his widow. So Henriette asked his friends what had happened, and they explained that Pierre must be dead, since their count had always come up short, and no one called Pierre's name when he counted noses.

Henriette shouted, "Pierre, open your eyes!"

"Have respect for the dead, you!" he warned. But he opened one eye.

Then Henriette said, "Go and stan' by your frien's, and let me count you-all."

"This no way to treat the dead," Pierre grumbled, "but I doin' it jus' to prove you a widow now, for true."

When the fishermen lined up, Henriette counted one-two-three-four-five-six.

They all exclaimed, "We six again!"

"Mebbe so," said Pierre stubbornly, "but how we know this number six who turn up so mysterious en't a stranger?"

Sighing, Henriette told the men, "When I point to you, each of you say your name."

"Jules."

"Jacques."

"Jean."

"Ti-Paul."

"Philippe."

"PIERRE! *C'est moi!* It is I! I got returnded from the dead!"

His friends gathered around him, crying how wonderful it was to have him back among the living. They thanked *le Bon Dieu*, the Good Lord, for this miracle.

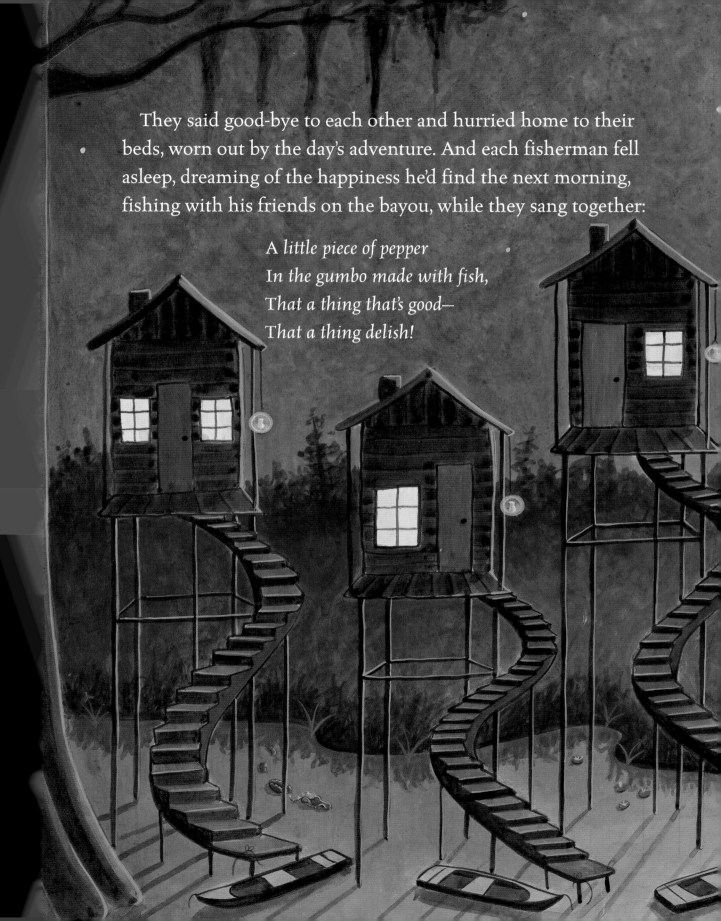

They said good-bye to each other and hurried home to their beds, worn out by the day's adventure. And each fisherman fell asleep, dreaming of the happiness he'd find the next morning, fishing with his friends on the bayou, while they sang together:

*A little piece of pepper
In the gumbo made with fish,
That a thing that's good—
That a thing delish!*

GLOSSARY

Barbue:	blue or channel catfish
C'est moi!:	It is I!
Grandmaman:	grandmother
Le Bon Dieu:	the Good Lord, the Kind God
Mais non!:	Oh, no! But, no!
Mes amis:	my friends
Pauvre:	poor
Pirogue:	a small, narrow rowboat—often, but not necessarily, a dugout
Sac-à-lait:	white perch, crappie
Ti:	little, small (from the French word "petite")

AUTHOR'S NOTE

Variants of this "noodle" story are well known, from Scandinavia to the Philippines. I have interwoven several of these tales, elaborating on the miscounting incident in particular. Since I have long been interested in Cajun culture, it seemed a logical step to set my retelling along the bayous of Louisiana, the heart of Cajun country. In fact, the six fishermen seem first cousins to the comic figure of Jean Sot, "Foolish John," whose misadventures, recounted by Cajun storytellers, have amused generations of listeners.

Those wishing to learn more about the Cajuns should refer to *The Cajuns: From Acadia to Louisiana*, by William Faulkner Rushton (New York: Farrar Straus Giroux, 1979) or *The Bayous of Louisiana*, by Harnett T. Kane (New York: William Morrow & Company, 1943). Excellent selections of regional folktales can be found in *Swapping Stories: Folktales from Louisiana*, edited by Carl Lindahl, Maida Owens, and C. Renee Harvison (Jackson: University Press of Mississippi in association with Louisiana Division of the Arts, Baton Rouge, 1997); *Cajun and Creole Folktales: The French Oral Tradition of South Louisiana*, collected and annotated by Barry Jean Ancelet (Jackson: University Press of Mississippi, 1994); and *Cajun Folktales,* by J. J. Reneaux (Little Rock, Arkansas: August House, 1994; also available on cassette from the publisher). See also *A Dictionary of the Cajun Language*, by Rev. Msgr. Jules O. Daigle (Ville Platte, Louisiana: Swallow Publications, Inc., 1984).

E

San Souci, Robert D.
   Six foolish fishermen

		DATE DUE	